Christmas Gala

Adult Naughty Tough Hard Extreme

Lana Kendra

it wasn't bought for your personal use only, go back to your favorite ebook retailer and buy your copy. Thank you for acknowledging this author's efforts.

Table of Contents

Content Warning

Due to its sexual content, this book is only for those over the age of legal adulthood. There are some topics with a lot of foul language. All of the characters are at least eighteen years old.

Introduction

Are you in search of an exciting and thrilling book to read? Look no further than this extensive collection of Erotic Suspense book. I offer a wide range of genres, including Romantic Erotica, Fantasy, and Urban BDSM Fiction, to cater to even the most discerning reader. Whether you enjoy Anthologies, Westerns, or Paranormal Romance, I have something to suit your taste. My collection also includes Poetic Folklore, Interracial, Black & African American Literary Criticism, and Gothic Horror for those who crave a deeper and darker reading experience. If you're interested in Futuristic, LGBTQ+, Short Stories, or Lesbian literature, my diverse range of options will keep you captivated. Additionally, I offer Humorous, Victorian, New Adult, and College Women's Psychological Mysteries for those seeking a lighter but equally engaging read. Furthermore, My Fairy Tale Collections,

Transgender, Contemporary Western, Bisexual, and Poetry genres will transport you to different worlds and explore a variety of themes. For my Teen and Young Adult readers, I have a selection of European Geography, Cultures, eBooks, Loners, Outcasts, Mythology, Folk Tales, and much more. With such a wide array of options to choose from, you'll never run out of thrilling and enchanting stories to immerse yourself in.

This is a story that will captivate your mind and turn on your fantasy gear for your long erotic desire. Enjoy the sexual tentions embedded in this story.

It is important to emphasize that this content is exclusively intended for individuals who are 18 years of age or older.

Christmas Gala

Laura had organized this grandiose Christmas gala for the neighborhood a week prior to Christmas. The main holiday celebration of the year was this one. It was intended to give the impression that the big media and social network firm she was employed by cared about people—even though it didn't. However, it was her responsibility as the company's head of public relations to slant the story and provide positive press.

It was time for some well-deserved publicity. Laura's company had been the government's main focus for the past year. They were held accountable for the falsehoods and misinformation that the nation was told. Thus, perhaps, this occasion might eclipse some of the negative coverage.

This time of year was particularly harsh for all of the city's underserved communities due to inflation and the recession. communities that are primarily minority. What better way to celebrate Christmas than in style?

Laura had meticulously prepared every aspect of the occasion. There would be giveaways, free food that was provided (and extra food that would be brought to households), musical acts, presents, and, of course, Santa!

She got a call less than two hours before the event began.

Calmly over the phone, the voice remarked, "Sorry, but the guy can't make it today. He's sick. We apologize for the late notice."

Laura said, trying not to show how annoyed she was. "OK. So send somebody else."

The voice went on calmly but remorseful, "Unfortunately, we don't have a backup available. It's a busy time of year and we're understaffed and fully booked."

"What the fuck do you mean?" Laura growled, showing her frustration.

"We're truly sorry. We can reschedule to another day. Free

of charge."

"I can't just reschedule. Our company planned the whole day around Santa coming. We have kids busing over as we speak."

The person on the other end of the line kept apologizing a lot and providing options. Laura sat back and attempted to settle herself, hardly paying attention.

Laura muttered to herself, "Fuck."

Her thoughts were racing with several situations. She told herself as she stabilized herself. They give me the huge dollars for this.

Laura was a recent hire. She was hired because of her prowess as a public relations whiz and business fixer. She was willing to take care of the mess in exchange for the big title and enormous sums of money they paid her.

Of all the CEOs, she was the youngest by a wide margin. Hated by all the women who believed she didn't deserve her position, she was adored by her male coworkers—especially the older, white men. This is due to the fact that she was constantly dressed to please and had supermodel-like looks in addition to her cunning and sharp mind.

All the men and ladies stared at her; she was always the focus of attention. Men would cinch their trousers at the sight of her physique.

She was confrontational, didn't take no for an answer, and created more enemies than allies. When necessary, she could entice and pander. understood how to play the game to achieve her goals. and didn't mind stepping on people's toes.

She thus caused a great deal of agitation in that executive suite simply by getting employed. Her opponents were also waiting for her to make a mistake.

Laura leaped out of her seat. She was going to get paid her huge salary in full.

The man started to ramble on the other end, but Laura cut him off, saying, "Can you at least give me a Santa suit?"

"Umm....yes, but we don't typically loan out suits without one of our trained actors. It's kind of a package deal." The tone bored her.

"Listen. You have 30 minutes to deliver a suit. Deliver it yourself. Throw it in an Uber. I don't give a fuck. But it better be here in half an hour." Laura yelled.

After hanging up, she hurried down the hallway in the direction of the elevator. Along the way, her pricey high heels make a clicking sound on the hardwood floor.

The doors of the elevator "dinged" open. A handful of her male coworkers glanced at her as they went by. Every time, they looked twice. Pressing the button for the lobby, she entered the elevator. There were still males in the elevator, and she could feel their stares burning a hole through her.

She dashed through the turnstiles and out of the elevator

as soon as it opened. Men tripped over each other to clear her path, and traffic parted for her.

At last, she discovered what she was searching for. Instead, it was who she sought.

Yashua Powerful.

He worked as an administrative front desk clerk in the lobby. Furthermore, he was ideal for Laura's needs.

Yashua was heavy and stocky enough to look like he had the Santa belly under the Santa costume. Laura recalled how excellent he was with guests, particularly young ones, on the occasions when the company sponsored "bring your kids to work" days. Furthermore, she had heard that he was simply working on this as a side gig in order to fulfill his desire to be an actor.

One small problem, though: he was Black. Laura skillfully framed it as a positive, saying that it was wonderful for the kids to perceive Santa as someone who was just like them.

especially in light of all the recent news reports about the biased corporate culture.

She told herself, "How could we be racist? We have a Black Santa!"

Shaken, Yashua said, "What do you want me to do?"

Laura said matter-of-factly, "I need you to dress up as Santa."

Yashua answered, "I can't do that. I don't even know what to do or say."

What's your name? "Act. Just do the same shit in the movies...""", "For Christmas, what would you like?", "Naughty or Nice"...be cheerful. Keep it corny and generalized," Laura attempted to allay his worries.

With hesitation, Yashua said, "I don't know. That's a lot to spring on me at the drop of a dime."

Laura batted her eyelashes and said, "I know, I'm sorry, but you'd be saving my ass, which would be a huge favor."

Yashua became excited at the prospect. He glanced at Laura's ass, which was curled up against the fabric of her garment.

That wasn't a secret. His biggest crush on Laura was on her. Would anyone not? She had an irresistible effect on him. Take a peek at her.

Laura had a toned body and was slender. quite tall for an Asian woman, rising to a height of about 6 feet in her absurdly high 4 1/2-inch heels. The ones with the crimson bottoms, the pricey ones, you know. Her face was exquisite, her skin flawless as porcelain. Her almond-shaped eyes mesmerized with a straightforward gaze. Her long, blond hair that had been dyed with black roots reached her mid-back. She was stunningly beautiful.

Additionally, the attire she wore to work ought to be illegal. They were sophisticated and fashionable, achieving the ideal mix of sexiness and professionalism.

She looked amazing today in a cream-colored turtleneck sweater dress. Her B cup breasts, her waist and hip contours, and the firmness of her lovely ass were all flaunted by the outfit. Her best feature, her long legs, were flaunted by the dress, which stopped about mid-thigh. His thoughts drifted to her legs, which were completely covered in sheer black stockings, pantyhose, or tights.

Then there were those heels—fuck me. Those heels, my goodness. Her feet were the ideal proportions for heels. Not excessively large or little. The ideal match for her lengthy legs. the ideal accent to her curvaceous body. The phrase "fuck me heels" must have originated with Laura, if there ever was one.

The absurd thing was that Laura always had this hot appearance. For Yashua, seeing Laura was the high point of the day. He jerked off to the countless images of her he had in his head. He believed Laura was unaware of his intense desire for her, but she was aware of it.

Laura batted her eyelids and came in close to give him a whiff of her enticing scent. "...please. Do it for the kids. For me."

"Okay, fine. But you owe me a date. Like a dinner. For real," Yashua snapped back.

With a playful smile, Laura said, "Let's see how good of a job you do...Black Santa."

Twenty minutes later, the Santa suit showed up. Delivered directly by the frightened customer support agent.

Everything happened just as expected. The children and their guardians experienced an incredible time. Meet Santa, take pictures, and tell him what they wanted for Christmas were all enjoyed by all. The children were thrilled to see a Santa who resembled them.

And it was killing Yashua. extroverted and upbeat around all the parents and children. You could have forgotten about some of your issues and felt the Christmas spirit since there was enough pleasure and laughter to go around.

Although Yashuta was chatting with the kids and taking pictures, she couldn't resist snooping a peek at Laura. He was making every effort to win her over. She looked so hot, damn it. He imagined that she was wearing the thigh-high stockings he was smitten with beneath her outfit. Subsequently, he had to interrupt himself, as he began to get an erection. It would have been unwise to do it when the children were sitting on his lap.

Laura saw how well Yashua was doing, despite the fact that she was juggling a million things. He was going to obtain his Christmas wish, and maybe even more, if he continued in this manner.

Following the children's time with Santa, Laura gave one of her staff members the order to announce the arrival of everyone and point them in the direction of the large company cafeteria located on the building's first floor.

With a ton of entertaining activities for the kids to enjoy, they transformed the first floor into a winter wonderland. All the traditional Christmas fare was prepared and served in the cafeteria. Laura also went above and beyond to make sure that toys and food would be delivered to the residences of the fortunate guests.

Laura had some things to tend to, so she gave her crew the order to take over in the cafeteria. She gave the order to send a few unfortunate subordinate associates who had to don Elves' costumes to supervise the remaining operations. She assured them that she would handle the cleanup here.

It was only she and Black Santa when they had all left.

Although Black Santa was perspiring under his disguise, he refrained from shaving until the final individual had departed. He was eager to return to wearing his regular clothing. Now that it was finished, though, he hoped he had done well enough to secure that date.

Laura stopped him as he started to undo the Santa suit's buttons.

"I need some pictures for marketing, so can you keep on the suit just a bit longer?" Laura said affectionately.

Yashua let out a sigh. He surmised that he wasn't yet.

Laura feigned tidying up while deliberately grabbing a few items, including a candy cane, a mistletoe, and one of the elves' hats. She also said aloud, "Thank you again. You were amazing."

"Whatever for the kids?" was Yashua's response. "It was pretty fun. I'm glad you convinced me to do it."

Laura laughed. "You must be tired. That was a lot of people sitting on your lap."

"I am pretty beat. It's really hot in this suit," said Black Santa with a smile.

Laura muttered. She said with a hint of coyness, "I've always loved the whole charade. Reminds me of being a child. Do you have time for one more?" pointing to Santa's chair.

Why not, Yashua reasoned. He did mind if Laura's luscious behind rested on his lap for an hour or two. He sat down and patted his calf.

Sexy as ever, Laura walked over to greet him. She tried to settle into his lap, but she ended up sitting directly between his legs on his crotch.

She stroked her ass over his dick with her back to him. She started to slowly rotate back and forth.

Black Santa's cock started to harden in his pants, and he could not contain his enthusiasm. Laura grinned as she realized.

In an attempt to gather himself, Santa cleared his throat before asking, "So, um, what can Santa do for you on Christmas pretty girl?"

She danced on his lap and said, "All I want for

Christmas...is a nice...LONG...vacation...somewhere far away...maybe a visit to the North Pole."

Santa Black swallowed. He was unable to come up with an answer.

Laura was still stroking his incredibly erect cock like a VIP stripper. His penis was at least nine inches long and thick, based on her estimation.

Tease him more, saying, "But I can't seem to find any flights." For added impact, she seemed to be upset.

With a cough, Black Santa said, "Well, um...maybe I can give you a ride on my sleigh."

With a smile, Laura said, "Really, Santa? Oh, I would be so grateful."

"But first, we have to check the list to see whether you have been naughty or nice?" improvised Yashua's actor.

"I'm always nice." Laura purred, looking astonished as she dry humped his engorged cock through his jeans.

"Um, is it Laura? Laura Chen. Oh yes, here I found you," Black Santa choked hard.

With a fake flip of an invisible book, Black Santa said, "...uh oh."

"What do you mean "Uh Oh"?" Laura asked, halting abruptly and humming his lap.

"Santa's list says you've been a very naughty girl," Black Santa went on.

Laura rubbed against his cock and said, "Oh no." "Does that mean I can't get my present?"

"Well there's still time before Christmas. You just have to be very good. Do something nice for others." urged Black Santa.

Laura got from his lap, leaving Yashua building a tent that was aching to be freed from its clothed prison. "Please Santa. I'll do anything." Laura said.

"First, you need to show some holiday spirit. You're not

wearing any Christmas colors," Black Santa said after giving it some thought.

Laura whirled, kicking up her pricey high heels. "The bottom of my shoes are red, does that count?"

Black Santa was able to get a clear view of Laura's gorgeous legs and her taut behind due to the abrupt movement. He never thought he would get to view them up close.

"That's a start."

Laura then leaned forward to give him a close-up view of her protruding round ass through her clothing. She moved a short distance away to the spot where she'd left the elf hat. With a seductive gesture, she reached down and put on the elf hat. She instantly changed into the most gorgeous Elf ever.

"How about this?" she jokingly inquired.

"That's better." Yashua agreed with an overly enthusiastic

nod.

Subsequently, Laura gave a small shake of her hips and raised her skirt to display her garter belt straps and the tops of her thigh-high stockings. They were both green in color.

"How about this? I'm wearing the green color of my Christmas stockings."

The first drops of precum oozed out of Yashua's cock at the amazing sight of Laura in thigh-high stockings.

True. Sure. You're feeling festive now." Black Santa yelled like a pastor.

With her high heels making a clicking sound with every step on the floor, Laura strolled slowly back over to Yashua, pushing aside her small little thong and rubbing her moist pussy for Santa to see.

"What more must I accomplish?She drooled.

Black Santa blinked sharply "Well, there's only so much Santa can't tell you. Certain things need to naturally come out of you; the Christmas spirit should originate from deep inside."

Laura feigned to ponder deeply as her eyes darted about the space, trying to find everything.

She continued, pointing to his cock and saying, "I love candy canes."

She discovered the one she had deliberately left on the ground and said, "I just love to suck on a candy cane."

She purposefully trod on the candy cane with her heel as she strolled over to pick it up, shattering it into pieces.

She picked it up and showed Black Santa all the broken parts enclosed in the little wrapping, saying, "Oh no...it's all broken."

"Oh, I think I found another one," she said, glancing across at his rock-hard cock that was still sticking out through his jeans. Is there a candy cane lurking in your slacks, Mr. Santa Clause?"

"Oh yes," Black Santa had to clear his throat. However, this sugar cane is unique."

Laura stepped in front of him, undoing the Santa costume belt and pulling down his pants, causing his enormous cock to finally burst out of its clothing cage. Laura measured the cock and it measured closer to 10 inches.

"Mmm...that looks delicious," Laura said, licking her lips. Please let me suck on that."

Black Santa unfastened his Santa blazer, pushed his slacks down to his ankles, and nodded excitedly.

Yashua leaned back, amazed at Laura's figure as she bent down in a standing stance with her body to his side. Laura thrust out her ass, arched her back, and leaned in close, grabbing hold of his cock and devouring it like the eager, greedy little slut she was.

Laura bobbed her head up and down on his massive cockhead, giving Black Santa a groan as the warmth of her mouth was beyond his wildest imagination.

Laura groaned, "Oh, I forgot how much I love the taste of a candy cane," in between slurps and licks. It's excellent. However, I've never had one that was chocolate."

Black Santa exhaled deeply and said, "Be sure to suck it good then. Acquire every inch. Melt it in your tongue."

Black Santa stroked against Laura's slick wet pussy as she continued to suck and spit on his erect cock, moving his hands along her tight body from her tits to her ass and finally below her dress. Laura went back to work on his cock with her mouth and tongue.

"This has to be heaven," Black Santa thought to himself, "or at least the North Pole."

With perfect accuracy, Laura worked his cock with her mouth and tongue, alternating between fast and slow speeds. She refused to come up for air, moaned and groaned on his cock, and with each suck, she moved her hand in a circular motion along his shaft.

Laura tickled the nerves on the tip of his cock with her tongue and hard suckles, then turned to lengthy deep sucks as she sought to get in as much cock as she could; the combination of good head and good jerk drove Yashua crazy.

Laura came up for air after spreading a decent layer of saliva on his cock for a few minutes, asking, "Have I been good enough now, Santa?"

Yashua gasped, "Almost..."

"What else have I got to do, Black Santa?" pouted Laura."

"I think it's time you go for a ride on the Polar Express," said Black Santa, nodding. I guarantee that you won't soon forget the experience."

Laura got up and slithered out of her panties, kicking them over to the side as they reached her ankles. "That's my favorite book."

After climbing up on top of Black Santa until she was straddling him with her legs on either side of his, she reached back and grasped his pulsating cock, which she then joyfully guided toward her aching pussy hole, taking a deep breath as she did so and pushing it inside.

Laura let out a loud moan the moment she felt the huge cock-head pierce through her pussy walls.

"Fuck" .

She had to ease into the size of his cock, which stretched her pussy open. She grimaced as she swayed her body slowly, up and down, coating his cock with her girl-cum with each motion.

one-inch increments.

She arched her back, pulled her body up till just the tip of his cock was still inside her, and then pushed down with all her power, until finally she was ready to take him all in.

"Fuck."

She pushed until all of his cock was buried deep inside of her; when it was, she screamed like a banshee and rode the Polar Express to its goal, cursing aloud at how deep he was.

Her mouth was open in a constant "O" shape, her hair was flying everywhere, she was pounding on his cock with reckless abandon, her screams and moans resonating through the walls as she slammed her body hard into his, making Santa's chair rock and scratch the floors with every bounce.

Black Santa was fucking so hard he could not stand it. He served only as her fuck-toy. Her erection rod. And he was perfectly fine being used.

"Yes, Mr. Santa Claus. Be a Jingle Bell Rocker. For Christmas, please give me those 12 inches." Laura let out a sultry bark.

At last, Santa had to stop and take a deep breath. "Damn, you gonna make Santa cum."

Laura leaped off, dropped to her knees, and gave his cock a fierce, intense suck. She gave him a violent jerk of the shaft.

Indeed, Santa. Give that cum to me. I'm seeing visions of a snowy Christmas. Let the snow fall all over my dirty face, please."

Black Santa got up and gave his cock a few slaps to make it go numb. No, not just yet. You still need to do more to get taken off the bad list.

Laura was told to kick her heels high in the air and lie back on the chair. Black Santa positioned his cock in line with her exposed pussy hole while her legs were spread wide. "Santa's getting ready to cum down the chimney," he bellowed, pushing past her and forcing his cock deep inside of her.

Laura's legs were seized by Black Santa, who rested each of her high-heeled shoes on a large shoulder. Then, he gave

Laura's pussy stroke after stroke of long dickering. He ensured she felt every bit of it.

As Laura's pussy opened wide for his massive cock, she was overcome with delirium. She pleaded with him to get into her. She reached over, picked up some mistletoe, and held it above their heads.

"Oh, you know what that means?" Laura scoffed.

Black Santa leaned close to her, kissing her. As tongues fluttered within one another's mouths, both mouths parted in lust.

Laura's legs slid down around his waist and encircled his powerful lower back, providing Black Santa with the ideal angle to give her a hard fuck. Black Santa really banged Laura's pussy with quick thrusts in and out of her juicy pussy hole.

As they continued to trade spit, Laura let out a loud moan into his mouth.

Then Black Santa broke off the kiss and used both hands to cup her ass-cheeks. His unique posture seemed like he shoveled his cock into her body, giving him the perfect angle to go balls within her, but he still thrust deep into her.

Laura was so ecstatically driven crazy by these long, deep strokes.

"My goodness. How do you do this? She exclaimed, "How are you doing that? "It is really amazing. Don't give up," she pleaded.

Black Santa continued to beat until Laura's body stiffened up, and he was more than delighted to oblige.

"Holy shit. I'm going to climax there, so keep going." Laura choked.

Black Santa was not going to quit, no matter how hard it tried. With every strong thrust, he let out a moan and a groan, and drops of sweat formed on his brow.

Laura erupted into a wave of orgasm, her legs flailing and

stiffening. Her whole body trembled and she let out repeated screams and moans.

White juices caked around Black Santa's cock shaft as he pulled his cock out of her pussy. Her asshole and pussy developed a layer of cream that trickled down his balls.

"Looks like it will be a White Christmas," he said, stepping back to admire his creation.

Laura continued to chew. She sat up and put Black Santa's cock inside her mouth once her orgasmic high subsided. She desired his Christmas in white.

She sucked his cock clean and proceeded to slobber all over it without any delay. With every slurp, she tasted her pussy secretions on his cock.

Laura came up for air and gasped, saying, "Now, I want you to create snow." I wish it were on my face. I want to eat it and taste it."

Not yet, said Black Santa, shaking his head from side to

side. One more task to complete."

For dramatic effect, he paused. "...I need you to lead my sleigh"

Laura was lifted from the chair by Black Santa, who then twirled her around. He forced her to widen her legs shoulder-width apart by pushing her forward. He entered her from behind, her pussy and ass opened wide to welcome him in.

He dove straight in, hitting her hard doggystyle, saying, "It's a long journey." We must travel quickly to the North Pole."

Laura shouted in delight as he hammered into her pussy. "Yes, make me ride your sleigh...make me take it."

With every thundering thrust of his pulse, his body crashed into hers, his balls slapping across her clit.

He looked to the side as Black Santa slammed furiously in to her pussy from behind. Conveniently, a false red nose was left behind. After gathering it up, he covered Laura's nose with it.

He took hold of her waist and used her body to brutally move her pussy back and forth on his long cock, saying, "Lead my sleigh Rudolph."

Now he had run out of puns.

Perhaps even one more, as Black Santa let out a yell of, "Oh fuck. It's Santa Clause time in the town. It's almost Christmas! Santa Claus is on his way."

When he extracted his cock, a tremendous rush heated up inside his balls and was about to burst out.

Like a ballerina, Laura pirouetted into position. his cock aimed straight at her face while she was on her knees. Her delicate hands found his cock and she jerked the cum to its rightful resting spot.

Black Santa let out a loud "FUCK" as the cum sprayed rope after rope across Laura's face, including her still-red nose. She attempted to catch as much cum as she could by sticking out her tongue and opening her lips wide.

When it was all over, Laura's face was covered in a thick layer of Santa's snow, which was gummy and sticky.

Yashua almost passed out as he fell into Santa's chair. His arse went slack and he began to breathe heavily.

Laura took the load in her lips and swallowed. Then she experimented with her hands and cheeks with the sperm. She licked her hands clean after shoving more of his sperm into her mouth. She cast a quick glance at Yashua's perspiring form.

"Mmmm....looks like I'm going to have to make this an annual tradition." Black Santa closed his eyes as Laura laughed.

"Merry Christmas to all and to all a goodnight."

Black Santa out til Christmas of next year.

Acknowledgments

The Glory of this book's success goes to God Almighty and my beautiful Family, Fans, Readers & well-wishers, Customers, and Friends for their endless support and encouragement.

About The Author

I've spent nearly a decade penning romantic novels. As a passionate writer of erotica, I craft dark, romantic erotica. Anime Naked Truth Se of Sacred Sexuality: Forbidden Seducing Short Stories of an Erotica Nude Sexy Girl Poster. Alongside Erotic Mystery Fiction, Victorian Erotica Sex, Black & African American Erotica, Euthanasia, Daddy Teaching, Forced Domination, Alpha Monster Cuckold, and BDSM for Adults, there's an Erotic Fiction in Kinky Family. I write dark, sensual romance because I adore the power of darkness and everything that it entails. Romance novels have always been my favorite kind of books, and now I'm writing them. The idea that you will like reading and enjoying my fiction as much as I enjoy pushing the frontiers of sexual pleasure in my writing thrills me more than anything else.